SA

To my mother and father

**Other Cambridge Reading books
you may enjoy**

Heroes and Villains
Edited by Tony Bradman

Letters to Henrietta
Nell Marshall

Sorcery and Gold
Rosalind Kerven

Sandstorm

Judy Cumberbatch
Illustrated by James Bartholomew

CAMBRIDGE
UNIVERSITY PRESS

Cambridge Reading

General Editors
Richard Brown and Kate Ruttle

Consultant Editor
Jean Glasberg

PUBLISHED BY THE PRESS SYNDICATE OF THE UNIVERSITY OF CAMBRIDGE
The Pitt Building, Trumpington Street, Cambridge CB2 1RP, United Kingdom

CAMBRIDGE UNIVERSITY PRESS
The Edinburgh Building, Cambridge CB2 2RU, United Kingdom
40 West 20th Street, New York, NY 10011-4211, USA
10 Stamford Road, Oakleigh, Melbourne 3166, Australia

First published 1998

Printed in the United Kingdom at the University Press, Cambridge

Typeset in Concorde

A catalogue record for this book is available from the British Library

ISBN 0 521 62927 6 paperback

Contents

CHAPTER ONE

Sandstorms creep up out of nowhere, turning the whole world upside down in a minute flat, blasting the insides out of you and curdling your brains. Sandstorms can drive you mad, said the old people in the village, and Rashida half believed them.

Rashida had been on her way home from school with Iman the day the storm blew up. They had taken the long way back, preferring the path which crossed the fields and then wound along beside the wide river. It was the middle of summer, and the sun boiled down out of a bright blue sky.

"It's so hot," Iman said, as they reached a small cluster of trees and paused. They always stopped here. It was the halfway mark between school and home. Near to them, a date palm stood, as straight and as tall as the minaret on a mosque, dwarfing the other trees nearby.

Rashida nodded. It *was* hotter than normal. She shifted her heavy school bag and squinted up at the sky.

"Let's stick our feet in the river," she said.

They squatted down on the bank and took off their sandals, then dangled their feet in the cool water.

Rashida lay right back and stared up into the tree where the green leaves grew out of the top of the trunk. A trail of red ants crawled slowly up the bark.

From the village, the sound of a car drifted over the fields, and then faded away, and silence fell again. ·

It was quiet, too quiet. As if the world had stopped.

Rashida closed her eyes and fell asleep.

When she woke, the world was going crazy.

It was almost dark, not black but a yellowy dark, the colour of sulphur. The sun had disappeared. A hot, dry wind was whipping across the water, swirling clouds of dust around her. She blinked, still half asleep, then leapt to her feet as she heard Iman yelling, "Wake up! Sandstorm!"

Rashida looked around her. They were well and truly caught. There was no time to get home. She could already feel the first grains of sand stinging her face and put her hand up to shield herself. "What are we going to do?" she shouted in a panic.

"We'll have to shelter here," Iman yelled over the mounting noise. "Hold on to the tree so you don't get blown away."

Rashida wrapped her arms around the trunk and pressed her face against the bark. The wood dug into her skin. She tightened her grip, fearful of being scooped up by the wind and hurled back to Abu Nuwaif.

The sand came over her in waves. It pounded her until she could hardly breathe and slashed her arms and legs, leaving her skin red and raw. There was sand in her clothes and in her hair. Her mouth and ears and nose were full of it.

She squeezed her eyes tight shut and huddled closer to the tree. The trunk swayed against her and the wind crashed through the leaves.

Then suddenly it was over.

One minute the world was going mad, the next it was as hushed as a school assembly with Abla Selma, the strictest teacher in the school, in charge.

Rashida cautiously opened her eyes, shaking her head to get rid of the sand. She straightened up slowly and wiped her face with the back of her hand.

"Iman," she croaked, her voice sounding strange in the sudden stillness. "Are you all right?"

There was no reply. Just a total silence, so complete that her voice died away to nothing and her feet made no sound as she moved across the ground.

Rashida stared round in panic. Iman should have been standing right beside her, at the next-door tree, but there was no sign of her at all.

"Iman," she called again. There was still no reply, just the deathly hush of the trees and the river that flowed by.

Rashida swallowed. Iman had disappeared as completely as if the wind had picked her up and tossed her into the water. Rashida started to rush towards the bank, trying to blank out the picture of Iman struggling in the river, then sighed with relief as she saw something move several metres away.

The dust still hung in the air, making it difficult to see clearly, but she could just make out a figure bent low beside the tall date palm. She moved towards it, then stumbled to a halt. She was near the figure now, and could see it distinctly in the gloom, scratching silently in the ground with its bare hands.

"Whatever . . ." Rashida started to say, then stopped, her eyes fixed on the hands. Thin and bony hands, like birds' claws. Not Iman's hands at all.

A twig snapped. Like a signal for the world to return to normal. The sound came back on. She could hear the water gurgling, leaves rustling and someone behind her shouting her name.

Rashida whirled round. Iman was standing several metres away, glaring at her through her thick, round glasses. "What are you playing at?" she snapped. "I've been calling you for the last five minutes."

Rashida gaped at her. "Iman," she gasped. "How did you get there? I . . ." She pointed to the palm tree, her voice trailing away in astonishment.

The air was clearing. Sun was beginning to filter through.

There was no-one there.

Rashida walked over to the tree and stared down at

the ground. The earth was undisturbed.

"But I saw someone," she said. "I know I did. She was digging."

Iman tapped the side of her head. "Mad," she said. "The sandstorm's made you see things."

Rashida started to turn away, then stopped. Something was poking up, close to the base of the tree.

"Come on," said Iman.

"Wait," Rashida said, as she scrabbled in the dirt. She pulled and the strange-shaped piece of wood came free.

Except it wasn't wood. Rashida knew that immediately. It had the heaviness of metal, and when she rubbed the dirt away, it gleamed like gold.

CHAPTER TWO

Rashida breathed a sigh of relief when she saw the small white house that stood beside the Blida road. It wasn't very grand, only four rooms in all, grouped round the courtyard, from where stairs led up to the flat roof. There was the small bedroom she shared with Grandma, and a kitchen and shower, and the salon they kept for visitors. Outside, hens scrabbled in the dust underneath the lemon tree.

Rashida ran forward, making the hens flap and squawk as they got out of her way, and burst in through the front door. Grandma was there in the courtyard, sweeping the floor. In her long black dress and faded pink shawl, she was as real and solid as a doum tree, and hardly faltered when Rashida threw her arms around her.

Iman had more brothers and sisters, and aunts and uncles, than you could count on both hands. Rashida only had her grandmother.

That wasn't strictly true. Rashida had family too, but they mostly lived in Cairo, and she didn't often see them. When Dad had died almost three years ago, Mum had gone to work in the city, and hardly ever came home.

Rashida had visited Mum once in the tiny crowded flat she shared with her sister's family, on the outskirts of Cairo. "It'll be better for you to stay with Grandma," Mum had said. "There's no room here." Rashida had looked round the balcony where they were standing, which her aunt used as a kitchen, and nodded. "You will visit me?" she had asked. "Of course I will," Mum had replied.

Rashida knew they needed the money, and how lucky Mum was to find a job. It wasn't bad living with Grandma. Rashida loved her more than anyone else in the world apart from Mum. But it didn't stop her wishing that things were different. That one day Mum would come home for good, and the loneliness Rashida felt would disappear.

"God knows best," Grandma would say when Rashida complained, but it was still hard, like now when it was so long since Mum's last visit. Longer than ever before.

Grandma straightened up and smiled, her face creasing into a thousand wrinkles.

"That'll teach you not to dawdle on the way home. I thought the sand ghouls had got you."

"Look," said Rashida, holding out the object. "I found it by the river, and thought I could clean it up."

"As if we haven't got enough cleaning to do after the storm," grumbled Grandma. "Put it down, and we'll look at it later."

It was getting on for evening when they finally sat down in the clean courtyard with a bucket of water and a scrubbing brush.

It took for ever to clean. They used sand and the pot scourer, and soap and water, and little by little the object began to take shape.

It was made of metal, with a large, flat round disc at one end and a long, thin handle. As Grandma polished it with a rag, it gleamed like gold in the afternoon sun, growing brighter and brighter, until it seemed like a pocket sun in itself.

"Well," said Grandma, as she passed it over. "That's no old bottle."

Rashida held it in her hand. Its surface was as smooth as glass, and the handle felt warm to the touch. She could see herself quite clearly, her curly brown hair, and the snub nose she wished were straight.

"It's like a hand mirror," said Rashida, "except it hasn't got any glass."

"And what do you think people did before they had glass?"

"Is it old?" Rashida asked.

Grandma took it from her and held it against her cheek for a second. A shadow passed over her face.

"I'm going to shut up the hens," she said, abruptly getting to her feet and handing the mirror back. "We'll talk about it later."

Rashida's eyes followed her as she walked outside. She frowned slightly, then turned back to the mirror. She twirled it in the sun, watching the way it caught the rays and reflected them on her face. She turned its smooth surface towards her again, then held it up in front of her face, and smoothed down her hair.

Her hand stopped halfway through her curls. The face staring back at her was all wrong. It wasn't hers.

This girl had long black hair falling straight down on either side of her cheeks and a straight fringe across her forehead.

And the saddest eyes Rashida had ever seen.

"Help," Rashida could almost hear her calling. "Please help."

Rashida blinked and shook her head slightly. But the girl gazed back at her.

The image was so clear that Rashida could see the flecks of the gold in her wide, green eyes. And the blue bead in the shape of a scarab beetle that was hanging round her neck.

As Rashida watched, the girl's eyes seemed to fill with tears, which spilt over and ran down her cheeks.

Without realising what she was doing, Rashida put out her hand to wipe them away. But it was cold metal she touched, not warm skin. And when she moved her hand away, the girl had vanished.

CHAPTER THREE

Rashida sat back on her heels, motionless for several seconds, staring into her own shocked eyes. Then she scrambled to her feet and raced outside.

"Grandma," she yelled. "Look at this."

She was halfway round the side of the house when she realised that Grandma was not alone. Leaning against the brick wall was the scrawny figure of Iman's Uncle Muhammed. He straightened up when Rashida appeared and stopped what he was saying.

Rashida jerked to a halt, waving the mirror at them. "I've just seen . . ." She tried to find the right words. "I've just seen –"

"Rashida," Grandma interrupted her sharply. "Where are your manners?"

Rashida gaped at her in surprise.

"Say hello to Ami Muhammed," said Grandma. "He's brought news from your mother."

"I'm sorry," said Rashida, holding her hand out in greeting. "I just . . ." She paused as Grandma's words sank in.

News from Mum.

It had been ages since they had last heard from her.

"Have you seen her?" Rashida demanded, turning on Muhammed. "How is she?"

"She's fine," Muhammed smiled.

"She's coming home next Saturday," said Grandma.

Rashida stared at her. "Next Saturday," she gasped.

"But that's less than a week away."

She looked from one to the other, suddenly aware of Muhammed, who was staring down at the ground, examining his toes.

She felt a tiny niggle of fear. It wasn't like him to be this quiet. Rashida liked him best of all Iman's uncles. He always joked, even when things went wrong, like breaking his leg, or crashing his bicycle. "What God wills," he would roar, waving his long arms in the air and bellowing with laughter.

Rashida glanced at him again, then up at Grandma, who was standing silently beside him. "Mum's not ill, is she?" she asked anxiously.

"Of course she's not," said Grandma. "Whatever gave you that idea? Now go and make Muhammed some tea before he dies of thirst."

Rashida put the mirror on the table in the kitchen and turned on the tap. Water splashed into the red teapot. She spooned in the tea automatically, and lit the gas.

She was being silly, she thought, imagining things that weren't even there, and forgetting the most important thing of all. Mum would be here in five days' time.

She smiled to herself as she thought about it. They'd go to the market together and out visiting. And in the evening they'd all sit round under the lemon tree, watching the stars come out and the moon rise.

It would feel just right. Her and Mum and Grandma together. Like they used to be.

She poured out two glasses of tea, picked up the

round tray and went outside.

"So what's all this I hear about your going mad in the sandstorm?" Muhammed asked.

Rashida grimaced. Trust Iman to go spreading tales.

"Sandstorms make me feel funny," she explained. She suddenly felt embarrassed about the figure in the storm and the face in the mirror. Tricks of the light, that's all they were. If she wasn't careful, people would be calling her crazy.

"Did Mum send any message?" she asked, changing the subject.

"Er . . . no," Muhammed said. "She just sent her love, and said she'd see you on Saturday."

Rashida gave a half smile. She hadn't missed the way he looked over at Grandma before answering, and the slight shake of her head in response. Rashida felt her sense of uneasiness return.

"I've got to go," Muhammed said suddenly, standing up. Grandma didn't try to stop him, even though he hadn't touched his tea.

Rashida walked with him to his heavy black bicycle, and watched him mount and pedal away. She stood looking after him for several minutes, then turned and followed Grandma into the house.

"What was it you wanted to tell me before?" Grandma asked.

Rashida looked at her, then shook her head. "Nothing," she said now. "Nothing important." She jerked her head towards the bedroom. "I'll go and do my homework," she said.

"Wait," Grandma called after her, but Rashida pretended not to hear her.

She dropped the mirror on the bed then walked over to the window and flung open the shutters. If she craned her neck, she could see the first stars shining in the night sky. She rested her cheek against the wall.

"Let Mum be OK," she begged silently, her fingers gripping the window ledge. "Please let her be OK."

Later that evening, when Rashida was clearing away the supper dishes, Grandma pulled out a letter from her pocket.

"Who's that from?" Rashida asked.

"Your mother," Grandma said. "Muhammed brought it, but I wanted to read it later when we were alone."

Rashida looked at the blue envelope. Her hands felt cold, and she carefully put down the glass she was holding on to the low wooden table, afraid that she would drop it.

"Come and sit down beside me," said Grandma, "and read me the letter." Rashida squatted on the floor beside her, and slowly took the letter.

"She's ill, isn't she?" she said. "Really ill. That's why you and Muhammed were acting so strangely."

It had been like that before Dad died. Whispers and people looking at her, and never really knowing what was happening.

Now she thought about it, it had been like that for months now, ever since Mum's last visit. There had been long, deep discussions between Mum and Grandma then, different from their normal conversations. And afterwards when Mum had gone back to Cairo, Grandma had seemed preoccupied for ages.

Rashida's hands trembled as she opened out the sheets of paper. She tried to read the writing but the letters got all jumbled up and danced in front of her eyes.

"Your mother's not ill," Grandma put her arm round Rashida. "She's getting married. That's all."

Rashida looked up at her. "What do you mean?" she asked.

"She's getting married," said Grandma, smiling.

"Married?" Rashida repeated. "Who to?"

Grandma fumbled with the envelope she was still holding and drew out a photograph and handed it to her.

It was a picture of Mum, wearing a dress Rashida had never seen before, all blue and yellow flowers with a large white collar. A tall, dark-haired man stood beside her, smiling into the camera. He was wearing a light brown suit and had a thin moustache.

"Is that him?" Rashida hesitantly touched the photo with her finger. It felt strange seeing Mum with a man like that. Not her dad but another man.

"His name's Sami," said Grandma. "He works with your uncle and has a good job. He's a court clerk. He'll look after your mother."

Rashida stared at the photo wordlessly, her mind a whirl.

"Is that why she's not been home recently?" Rashida asked finally, relief gradually turning to anger.

"Partly," said Grandma.

"Why didn't you tell me?"

"We were waiting for things to be arranged," said Grandma.

"We!" Rashida bit her lip. She could feel tears in her eyes, and blinked them away. So, Grandma had known all along and never said anything. It made it worse; made it seem as if she didn't matter at all.

"You'll meet him on Saturday," said Grandma. "He's coming with Mum."

Rashida turned rigid.

"It's not fair," she burst out. "She hasn't been to see me for months, and now she's only coming because of him."

"You know that's not true," Grandma said. "Your mum loves you."

"Then why does she want to marry again?"

"It's a long time since your father died," said Grandma.

"You never married again," said Rashida, turning on her. "There's no law that says you have to marry again."

Rashida didn't wait to hear any more. She turned and ran away before Grandma could stop her, out into the darkness and along the path that led to the tall date palm.

She flung herself down on the ground, and leant back against the tree, tears streaming down her cheeks. Above her, the leaves whispered and she could hear the faint rush of water.

Once she'd stood beside the tree with Mum, before she'd gone back to the city, and Mum had said, "I'll stand on the bridge in the centre of Cairo and look down at the river, and I'll know it's flowed right past here."

That was all gone now, all finished.

Rashida knew it was wrong, but as the ache inside her grew so sharp that she could barely breathe, she curled up close to the tree and wished fiercely that Sami were dead.

CHAPTER FOUR

Rashida lay on her bed on Wednesday afternoon, listening to the bang of Grandma's aluminium pan and the hiss of the primus stove as she heated water for the washing. Friday was the usual day for washing clothes, unless Grandma was upset, like now. Then she did it whenever she pleased.

Rashida sighed. It was hot and stuffy in the small bedroom and she half wished she were outside with Grandma. But Grandma wanted to talk, and Rashida couldn't. Not yet. She turned over her pillow, hoping it was cooler on the other side, and felt the brush of metal.

The mirror gleamed dully. She'd forgotten all about it, and now she picked it up, still half asleep, half full of dreams.

It was like another dream, fuzzy at first, a blur of a dark room and a figure seated on the floor.

The reflection wavered and then cleared, grew so sharp that she could see the pots standing in rows, could smell the smoke wafting through the door and an acrid sourness, too, that she didn't recognise. And from nearby, the sound of angry voices and the feeling of fear.

The girl sat with her back to the wall, listening to the pounding feet outside and the confused jumble of voices.

She carefully filled a pot with the sour-smelling dough, coughing as a wave of smoke drifted in from the oven, her ears straining to hear what was going on outside. *Even Opet, her father's cousin, who worked with her, had stopped talking, stopped her constant angry complaining about her feet and her back and the laziness of the other workers.*

The noise from the street grew louder.

The girl stood up and went to the window. She could see a crowd gathering outside, near the carpenter's shed where her father worked. For a moment, she imagined him bending over the coffin he was carving, smiling as he rarely did at home, now that her mother had left them for the Underworld.

The crowd of people parted and fell silent as a tall man elbowed his way to the front. She recognised him. It was Nakhte the chief scribe, and he was followed by the medjay-police. They walked past the bakery and on towards the carpentry shed.

"What's the matter?" asked the girl.

"The tombs have been robbed," said Opet. "They are going to arrest the thief."

The girl shivered, despite the clammy warmth of the bakery.

"What's your father been doing?" Opet nudged her as the scribe made his way into the carpenter's workshop. "Not robbing the dead, I hope." She sniggered at her own joke.

The girl turned away. Sometimes she hated Opet. A stir of excitement among the crowd made her look up again. The medjay-police had re-appeared, pushing a man in front of them.

The girl craned her neck to see better, then cried out in dismay.

It was Ani, her father, and he was being held like a prisoner.

"What is it? What are they doing with him?" she gasped.

"They say your father's a thief," said Opet, her eyes gleaming maliciously. "They say he's broken the seal of the dead and stolen from the tombs."

The girl shrank back.

"No," she screamed. "It's not true, it's not true."

The screams died away. Rashida lay petrified. She was panting as if she'd been running and her long cotton gallabia was soaked through with sweat.

Then her sight cleared. The room swung back into focus. There was Grandma's nightdress hanging on the wall, and the prayer mat rolled up in the corner.

She jerked the mirror towards her again and tried to see through its bronzy brightness. But this time, it told her nothing and kept its secrets to itself.

Rashida jumped off the bed and raced outside. Grandma was bent over the large washing bowl full of soapy water.

"Whatever's the matter?" she asked. "You look as if you've seen a ghost."

Rashida thrust the mirror into her soapy hand.

"I saw a face," she stammered, "but it wasn't mine."

Grandma held the mirror quite steady. Over her shoulder, Rashida could see the reflection quite clearly, the pink scarf knotted on top of her head, the wisps of grey hair peeping out from underneath and the deep furrows between nose and mouth.

"It looks like me," Grandma said finally, smiling up at her.

"But it was all so real," Rashida explained. "There was a girl, and people shouting, and I felt so frightened."

Grandma put her hand out and drew her towards her. Rashida leant on her shoulder, breathing in the dusty smell of her old black dress.

"I expect it was just a dream," said Grandma. "Some dreams get so tangled up with what's happening that they seem real."

Rashida sat in silence for a time, watching Grandma's slightly swollen hands rub and squeeze the clothes, dip and rinse and squeeze again. She might be 70 years old, but she had the strongest arms of anyone Rashida knew. She could take the whole of a wet sheet and squeeze it till the very last drop was gone.

"You can't keep the mirror, you know," said Grandma, breaking into her thoughts. "Not if it's old. You'll have to hand it to the authorities. I don't want any trouble with them."

Rashida gripped the mirror tightly.

"We don't know it's old," she said. "Please, Grandma. Let me keep it a bit longer."

After a moment, Grandma nodded.

"A bit longer," she said. "Now go and hang these clothes out or they'll never get dry."

CHAPTER FIVE

Rashida overslept the next morning. Weird dreams of Mum and Sami had chased her through the night and, somehow muddled in them all, a girl had shouted, "It's not true. It's not true."

By the time she reached school, she was hot and dusty. The bell had gone and the only person around was Hagga Miriam, who was sitting in her usual place under the mango tree by the school gate. She had a basketful of peanuts beside her, which she sold in break time. She nodded at Rashida, as she walked past into the empty playground. "Ta'akharti," she said unnecessarily. "You're late."

Rashida sighed as she crossed the sandy netball pitch towards the long, single-storey, brown building.

She wished her classroom wasn't right at the end of the long covered verandah. Through the open windows of the other classrooms, she could see the rows of girls in their blue tunics and trousers, their faces framed in white head scarves, their eyes following her as she walked past.

Abla Selma was waiting for her, as thin and bony as a skeleton. As Rashida came through the door, she tapped the table in front of her with a ruler.

"Rashida Hassan," she snapped. "All behind like the cow's tail, as usual."

Someone tittered. Rashida flashed a furious glance towards the back of the class as she headed for the desk she shared with Iman.

"History," Iman muttered, out of the side of her mouth. "Page 63."

Rashida opened the dog-eared book, which had its cover missing, and leant back in her seat, watching a fly circling near the window. Abla Selma was drawing pyramids on the blackboard and droning on about 'our great Egyptian heritage'. Rashida caught Iman's eye and smiled slightly.

Mum sometimes referred to her as 'mad Abla Selma' because she was so crazy about the past. She would go on and on and on about history given half the chance. Iman reckoned the worst punishment she could imagine would be to be locked up with Abla Selma in a museum.

Rashida could never make up her mind about the teacher. When Dad had died, she remembered how Abla Selma had talked straight to her, not hidden things or been embarrassed like everyone else. It was as if she had understood how Rashida felt and knew what it was like for her.

But she wasn't often like that. Most times she was as sharp as glass and the strictest teacher in the school. Iman hated her, wished she would bury herself with the mummies she was always going on about. Rashida wasn't so sure.

She yawned. She could vaguely hear the teacher in the background talking about Ancient Egyptians and temples. Her mind wandered back to Mum. In a couple of days, she would be here with Sami. The idea still filled her with dread. She looked sideways at Iman, wondering if she knew about Sami and Mum yet.

Tombs . . . temples . . . Abla Selma's voice broke into her thoughts. She tried to push the words away, but they niggled at the back of her mind.

Tombs . . . temples . . .

She jerked upright in her seat, suddenly concentrating on what Abla Selma was saying.

"Rameses II was among the greatest of the Pharaohs. Among the major legacies of his reign was the temple at Thebes."

Rashida slumped back in her chair. It had been a crazy idea. She idly turned the pages of the book, vaguely taking in the blurred black and white photographs of pyramids and statues. The colour plates were in the middle of the book. She'd seen them hundreds of times before. The Sphinx and Luxor, Tutankhamun and a painting from one of the tombs.

She was just about to turn the page when she stopped,

her eye caught by a figure in the top left-hand corner.

It was the picture of a girl. She was painted sideways on, her body in profile. She wore a rich yellow striped dress and her hands were outstretched, clasping a plate of flowers and food.

But it was the face that fascinated Rashida: the long, straight black hair, and fringe cut straight across, and the eyes outlined with black kohl.

Rashida shivered. She could feel the hair rising on the back of her neck, and her hands had gone cold and clammy.

It wasn't the girl from the mirror. Too old for one thing and too grand. But it was like her.

Rashida feverishly turned back to the other photographs. She stared down at the painted coffin, then at a model of a bakery. The wooden figures were tiny. She could barely make out what they were doing. She glanced down at the inscription, but she didn't have to read it. She knew what it would say. She knew how they'd made bread in Ancient Egypt. She'd seen them.

Rashida swallowed, her mouth dry.

She forced herself to stay calm. She was imagining it all. She had remembered this picture from school, and had had a dream about it. That was all. It was easily explained.

All the same, Rashida couldn't wait to get out of school to look at the mirror again. It was sitting in her school bag right now, where she'd put it so that she could show Iman. She reached down to touch it, and felt Iman's elbow jab her in the ribs.

She looked up with a start to find Abla Selma standing beside her, waiting for an answer.

"I . . . er," Rashida mumbled, looking over at Iman for help.

"Since you obviously find these pictures more interesting than my lesson, you can study them in detention," said Abla Selma.

"Cow," Iman mouthed. Rashida grinned half-heartedly.

The bell went for the end of lessons. It took about a minute for the classroom to clear. Rashida sat alone at her desk, watching the girls stream out in a chattering mass into the playground and gradually disappear in the direction of the school gates.

"Read the chapter on Rameses II," Abla Selma ordered sharply, her mouth compressed into a thin scarlet line. She took out a pile of books and started marking.

Rashida considered telling her that she hadn't slept properly the night before, and had problems at home. But the teacher looked so forbidding that she quickly decided against it.

Instead she pulled the book towards her and opened it at random, pretending to study it. Words and drawings danced before her eyes. After a minute, she squinted up at Abla Selma, then carefully slid her school bag towards her. She could feel the mirror through the pink, striped cotton of the bag. She hesitated.

Abla Selma slashed across a page with her red pen.

31

The playground was emptying fast, but the screech of voices still drifted in through the window.

Rashida drew a deep breath then dragged the mirror out onto her lap. She didn't have long to wait. It lay for a moment, dull and opaque in the shadow. Totally lifeless.

Then it began to change.

Rashida watched in fascination as her image grew fuzzy and broke up. Her hand trembled slightly and prickles of fear ran down her spine. It was too late to stop now, impossible to look away. From far off, she heard someone scream and felt the cold stone of a wall scraping across her back.

The girl squeezed closer to the wall. Her legs were tired from standing for so long and her head throbbed.

She looked ahead again. The judges sat circling her father, serious, grim-faced. Her father, who was so brave he hunted among the crocodiles and didn't flinch if a snake crossed his path.

The questions started again.

"Why were you by the tomb that night?"

"I wasn't," Ani's voice broke.

For a moment, the girl thought he was going to fall down. But he recovered himself.

"I was praying late in the temple, then I went home."

The head of the medjay-police held up an object.

"This is an amulet inscribed with the names of one person, 'The painter, Ani, son of Kai.' Do you recognise it?"

Ani put his hand to his neck, and frowned. "It's

mine," he said. "Where did you find it?"

"It was found inside the entrance to the tomb. Can you explain that?"

The girl gasped. She had to lean forward to hear her father speak above the uproar. He shook his head.

"I don't know how it got there," he said, after a moment.

"Tell us where you have hidden what you stole."

"I can't. I didn't steal anything."

"Tell us, or we'll have to beat the truth from you."

Ani was silent. The headman nodded to a large man who was standing nearby.

The girl clenched her hands, her eyes fixed on the long stick which the man was carrying. He moved slowly towards her father, and raised his arm.

The girl shut her eyes, put her hands over her ears, but she couldn't shut out the sound, the swish of the stick as it rushed through the air and the thud as it landed.

She dug her knuckles deeper into her ears and squeezed her eyes tighter, but through it all, she could hear the moans of pain, and the sharp indrawn breaths of the spectators; through it all, the steady swish and thud, swish and thud. She was trembling now. Tears trickled down her cheeks and she murmured again and again, "Stop, stop, stop."

Rashida stared at the ink-stained wood of her desk in confusion, her mind a blur of faces and sounds.

"Rashida Hassan."

She became aware that someone was calling her. She raised her head and saw Abla Selma coming towards her.

"Why were you talking to yourself?"

"I wasn't. I was reading out loud," muttered Rashida, as she hastily pushed the mirror back into her bag.

Abla Selma's eyes bored into her. Almost as if she knew. Rashida's hand clenched over her bag, her heart thudding so loudly that she was sure the teacher could hear it.

Then Abla Selma turned round and went back to her marking. Rashida let out a silent breath and glanced down at the page open in front of her. There was a picture of an animal which had the body of a lion and the head of a crocodile, with its jaws wide open. She recognised the picture. It was the monster Ammit, whom the Ancient Egyptians believed ate up the hearts of the dead.

Rashida shivered. She had to tell someone or she would explode. She glanced through the window but the playground was empty. Iman had gone home without her.

CHAPTER SIX

The mirror banged against Rashida's leg as she walked slowly along behind Grandma the next morning. They were on their way to the souk. It was Friday, no school day, and they were going to market together.

This was usually Rashida's favourite part of the week. People came into the village from the surrounding hamlets, and the square in front of the mosque was packed with stalls. Dozy Abu Nuwaif was suddenly alive with colour and noise.

There was everything on sale: onions, cabbages and spinach, long, green beans and baskets of potatoes; boxes of eggs and slabs of salty, white cheese; buckets of black olives, and green and orange pickles. Then there were the pedlars who came from Cairo, with their carpets and jewellery and pots and pans, and the old lady who sold charms to keep away the devil.

But today was different. Today Rashida had other things to think about. Too much to think about. There were Mum and Sami, as if she could forget. But even they were unimportant compared to this. She looked around. All she wanted was to see Iman, to have her look at the mirror and tell her she wasn't going mad.

"Come on," said Grandma. "Everything will be gone if we don't hurry up. And we've got so much to get, with your mother arriving tomorrow."

Rashida walked faster. The mirror bumped against her. "Please let Iman be there," she prayed silently.

Abu Nuwaif was already crowded. The main street leading to the square was full of cars and carts and donkeys and bicycles, and long before they reached the market, Rashida could hear the cries of the stall-holders.

Grandma sailed along, basket perched upon her head. "Sabah al Khair. Marhaba." The sing-song greetings passed over Rashida's head as she followed behind, scanning the faces of everyone she met.

"Beautiful ripe tomatoes," yelled an old man, wearing a round, white hat. "Only thirty piastres."

Grandma stopped and slowly bent down, squeezing and fingering the tomatoes. "As rotten as they come," she said, as one burst in her hand.

She moved along the long line of stalls, inspecting, fingering and bargaining to the very last piastre. Sometimes Rashida wished that Grandma was not quite so like Grandma.

Rashida fidgeted, looking for Iman. Grandma was examining eggs now, testing them for hairline cracks in a bowl of water, and protesting loudly at the price.

Rashida turned away. She searched the rows of shops that lined the square. Anwar, the tailor who sat crouched over his sewing machine, bales of blue and pink cloth piled crookedly around him. Farooq's, the hardware shop, with its buckets and pans, brooms and kettles.

"Rashida," Grandma tugged at her hand. "Stop dreaming and put the eggs in the basket."

Then Rashida saw Iman. She was standing on the corner, by Ami Salim's shop, holding her baby brother.

"I've got to speak to Iman," said Rashida, dashing off through the crowd before Grandma could stop her.

"What's the matter?" Iman protested, when Rashida dragged her round the corner and into an alley.

Rashida pulled the mirror out of her bag and thrust it into her hand. "Look," she said. "This is what I found in the sandstorm."

"Wow," breathed Iman. "What is it?"

"It's a mirror," said Rashida. "Hold it up in front of your face." She held her breath, watching Iman closely, waiting for the start of surprise, the sudden stillness, the 'I don't believe this' look.

A car tooted, and the Blida bus rumbled up the main street, belching grey smoke. Vaguely, Rashida registered Abla Selma waiting to cross the road, looking closely in their direction. She turned back to Iman. If only Iman could see the girl too, she thought, then she would know she wasn't going mad.

"Well," she asked, when she couldn't stand the waiting any longer, "can you see anything?"

"It's a bit blurred for a proper mirror," said Iman as she handed it back. Rashida took it, the disappointment so sharp that she could almost taste it.

"Didn't you see anything?" she asked again.

Iman's brother started to wail, and she put him down on the ground.

"Like what?"

"People?" Rashida asked before she could stop herself.

Iman pushed her spectacles up her nose and gave her a strange look. "Of course not," she said dismissively. "Whatever made you ask that?"

"Just an idea," Rashida muttered.

"It'll be all right, you know," Iman said. She looked embarrassed as soon as she'd spoken.

"What do you mean?" Rashida asked.

"About your mum." Iman picked up her brother. "I mean, you've been acting a bit weird. I thought –"

"I'm fine," Rashida said, before Iman could finish.

She shoved the mirror into her bag and slung it over her shoulder. It felt as heavy as a hundred kilos of bricks. "I've got to go," she said, turning away. "Grandma will be waiting for me. There's a lot to do before tomorrow."

CHAPTER SEVEN

Mum had already arrived when Rashida got back from school on Saturday.

She heard voices as soon as she entered the house. Her mother's laugh and the deep, barking voice of a man.

She walked slowly across the courtyard to the room at the far end, her eyes fixed on the large, shiny brown shoes that were outside the door, beside her mother's sandals. She slipped off her own sandals and went inside.

"Rashida," Mum exclaimed. "Here you are at last."

She was sitting beside Grandma on the pink-covered mattress that ran all along the back wall. Her bracelets jangled as she held out her arms and Rashida ran to her, suddenly pleased to see her. It was good to smell her perfume again, nice to feel her dangling earrings brush her cheek. She was wearing the same dress that she'd worn in the photograph, and her brown hair was cut differently.

She seemed younger and less tired than Rashida had seen her look for a long time. She even had lipstick on.

"You've grown again," said Mum, holding her tightly, "and you're so thin. Isn't Grandma feeding you properly?"

"Of course she is," Rashida said.

"I was only joking," said Mum, smiling across at Grandma. She turned Rashida round towards the man who was getting to his feet.

"This is Sami," she said.

The man smiled, showing a mouth full of bright, white teeth. He towered over Rashida, and she shrank back against Mum, feeling scared of him. He looked so strange in his trousers and shirt and bright blue tie. The men in Abu Nuwaif wore striped gallabias and sandals on their feet.

"What a lovely girl," Sami said. "You're just as beautiful as your mother said you would be."

There was an awkward silence. Rashida stared across at the large black and white photograph of Grandfather Ibrahim looking down from the wall opposite, and tried to think of something to say.

"We've got something special for you." Sami picked up a box and handed it to her.

Rashida took it, her heart sinking.

"Well, aren't you going to open it?" asked Mum, linking arms with Sami and smiling at her.

40

Rashida picked at the blue and pink paper wrapping, and stared at the china doll that emerged, looking like a blonde-haired monster.

"Thank you, Ustaz Sami," she managed to say, screwing her face into a tight smile. "It's lovely."

"Call me Uncle," said Sami. "We're soon to be family."

There was another short silence. Grandma heaved herself to her feet, and collected the glasses from the table. She motioned to Rashida to sit down, and left the room.

The silence lengthened. Rashida felt as if her tongue had got stuck in her throat. From the kitchen came the clatter of the dishes.

"How are you getting on at school?" asked Mum. "How's Abla Selma? She's Rashida's teacher," she explained to Sami.

"Fine," said Rashida shortly. She wasn't going to talk about problems at school in front of Sami. She wished he'd take his horrid doll and disappear, leaving her and Mum alone.

"Let's see what you're doing now." Mum sounded nervous, and her hands shook slightly as she pulled Rashida's school bag towards her.

"Wait," Rashida tried to stop her, but it was too late. The exercise books came slithering out, and the mirror dropped to the floor.

"Whatever's this?" Mum leant forward to pick it up. The sun's rays caught it, and for a brief second the mirror gleamed like fire.

"Let me see that." Sami suddenly shot out a hand and grabbed it from her.

He was kneeling directly in the path of the sun. The light hit his face and, for a moment, Rashida wondered if she had seen him before. The flecks of dust danced around his hands as he twisted the mirror to catch the light, and his fingers traced the mirror's outline.

"It's lovely," he murmured, half to himself. Then he swivelled round to face her. "Where did you get it?" he demanded.

Rashida gulped, hating the sight of his hands touching her mirror.

"I bought it." The words were out before she could stop them.

"Where? In a shop . . . the market . . . where?" Sami fired the questions at her, one after another.

"What's the matter?" asked Mum, touching his arm. "You sound quite excited."

"I thought it was old," he said.

Mum looked worried. "It's not, is it?" she asked, turning to Rashida. "Where did you get it?"

"It's just something they make for tourists," she said. She could feel herself going red. She hated lying to Mum. "I bought it in the market."

"I'd like to get one," said Sami. "You'll have to take me to the shop."

"You can't," Rashida said. "I . . . I mean it was the last one."

"Was it?" asked Sami. "Never mind."

Their eyes met.

Rashida looked away quickly. He knew she was lying. She could see it in his face.

She stretched out her hand and, after a second's pause, he returned the mirror to her.

Rashida put the mirror back in her school bag. Her hands were as cold as ice, and she realised that she was frightened. She hugged the bag against her.

For some reason she didn't want Sami to touch the mirror again.

"He could be worse," Iman pointed out to her that evening. "He could have boils."

Rashida smothered a giggle, and tried not to spill the tea she was measuring into the bright red pot that was sitting on the flames. From across the courtyard came the babble of voices and the sound of laughter.

Half the village had been visiting, to say hello to Mum or, more likely, to get a look at Sami. Even during Eid feast, Rashida thought, there never were this many visitors. Her arms ached from having carried round trays of tea and coke right through the afternoon.

She started arranging a fresh lot of glasses on the tray and spooned sugar into each one.

"Just think," Iman went on. "He could pick his nose, or smell, or be fat and old like Mariam's stepfather. *He's* over 70."

Iman was trying hard. Rashida half smiled. But then the sound of more laughter from outside made her grit her teeth again. "He's got sweaty palms," she said, "and I don't trust him."

She picked up the tray and walked to the salon. The room was still crowded. There was Iman's mother, cradling a baby, and Iman's two fat aunts. Ami Salim's wife and Abla Fawzia were there, and even Abla Selma had walked over from school with another teacher.

Sami turned and looked at Rashida as she came in and Rashida wondered if he'd heard what she'd just said to Iman.

"Abla Selma's been telling Sami about the history of Abu Nuwaif," said Mum, with the suspicion of a wink, as Rashida handed round the glasses.

"The museum's very interesting," said Abla Selma, in her clear, precise voice, "and of course, there's the temple as well."

"Don't encourage him," Mum said. "He thinks he's an antiquities inspector. He'd only been here for five minutes this morning when he thought he'd found a priceless antique."

As she said this, she leant forward, and Rashida saw with horror that she had picked up her school bag, which was lying under the table. Before Rashida could stop her, she pulled the mirror out of the bag and waved it over her head.

"Pure gold, you see." She laughed, moving the mirror, so that it glinted in the light.

Rashida clenched her hands tightly in her lap. She glanced anxiously round at the circle of faces.

A slight breeze stirred, making the light bulb swing. The faces gleamed palely, Sami smiling slightly, Iman frowning, Grandma staring down at the ground and Abla Selma with her mouth open.

"What is it?" Iman's mother asked.

"Something Rashida picked up in the market for 100 piastres," Mum said, and everyone roared with laughter.

Rashida forced herself to smile. She could feel Iman's puzzled eyes resting on her. Across the room, Grandma stirred restlessly. Her lips were pinched together and when she looked up, Rashida could see the anger in her face. Their eyes met. Rashida made a tiny sign with her head, silently begging her not to say anything. Grandma stared at her, then seemed to nod, and Rashida sighed with relief.

They were passing the mirror round. Rashida watched it being handed from person to person. Abla Selma had it now. She held it close up to her face, and ran her fingers over it. In the flickering light, her hand seemed to shake. The seconds dragged by, then Mum reached over and took the mirror back from her and returned it to Rashida's bag.

There was a general buzz of conversation. Sami leant over to stub out his cigarette in the ashtray on the table.

"I thought it was Ancient Egyptian at first," he said, suddenly, his voice cutting through the chatter. "There's something similar in the Cairo Museum."

Rashida jerked upright, aware of everyone looking her way again.

Then Mum laughed. "Don't go round telling people that," she said, "or we'll have the police breathing down our necks. You know what the penalties are for not reporting antiquities."

"We've got to do our homework," Rashida said, moving to the door. "Coming, Iman?"

"Why did you tell them you bought it?" Iman asked, immediately they were out by the lemon tree.

"Ssssh." Rashida glanced nervously over her shoulder. "Look, I want you to promise not to say anything about me finding it."

"But why?" Iman said.

"Because Sami will only go thinking it really is old and take it away from me," Rashida said.

"But supposing it is?" Iman said, her eyes scared. "You could be put in prison. You heard what your mum said."

"It's mine," Rashida said shortly. "Sami's got no right to come here telling me what to do with it. Promise you won't tell?"

"But . . ." Iman started, then stopped. "OK, I promise," she said.

Rashida sighed. That just left Grandma.

She had to keep the mirror safe. She wasn't sure why yet. She just knew.

CHAPTER EIGHT

Rashida stared up at the moon glowing down out of the silver-specked sky, and listened to the faint rustle of Mum in the other bed. They were sleeping on the roof, where it was cooler.

When Mum came home, this was the time Rashida liked best. They would climb up to the roof together and lie awake, giggling and chatting like two schoolgirls.

But not tonight. Tonight they were more like a couple of strangers.

"You will try and like Sami, won't you?" Mum suddenly whispered.

Rashida stiffened, and pretended to be asleep. The silence stretched between them like a huge, gaping hole, until finally she heard Mum sigh and turn away.

Rashida glanced over at her and thought of the photo hanging on the wall in the sitting room. She knew it off by heart: Dad standing behind Mum with one hand on her shoulder and, between the two of them, Rashida in her best dress with a white ribbon in her hair. "Say 'cheese'," the photographer had said, and they had all laughed at the funny English word and the camera had clicked. Now Dad was gone and Mum was leaving too.

Rashida shifted her leg and felt the mirror underneath the sheet. She had hidden it there, to keep it from Sami's prying eyes. He might be staying in the hotel, but not one corner of the house was safe from him.

It was quiet. She could hear the steady rumble of Grandma snoring downstairs. And, after a time, Mum's soft, even breathing. She was asleep.

Rashida slipped her hand under the sheet and pulled out the mirror. She traced the curve with her fingers, and felt the sharp, pointed end of the handle with the tip of her thumb. She sat up and held the mirror upright in the moonlight. It gleamed like silver, a pocket moon instead of a pocket sun, drawing in the light and throwing it back at her.

Thousands of years old, she thought as she watched her ghostly reflection. Could it really be from Ancient Egypt, like Sami had said?

Then the light began to change. The low wall seemed to melt in front of her and the sky caved in. Rashida clutched the mirror, her eyes fixed on the faces now looming out of the shadows. She tried to look away but she was being drawn in, deeper, deeper. And the night shadows filled with the sound of a man sobbing.

The girl kept her eyes looking straight ahead, on a point just above the head of the scribe, and waited. Beside her,

Opet fidgeted. The room was silent, except for her father's hoarse breathing and the scratching of the scribe's pen on the papyrus.

Then the priest stood up. She watched as his mouth started to open. He was so close she could see his blackened teeth and the pink of his tongue.

"Read the charge, and the sentence," he told the scribe.

"Ani, you have been tried for breaking into and stealing from the tombs, and have been found guilty." Nakhte's deep voice echoed round the packed room.

Guilty.

"No!" The scream was somewhere in her head, lost in the roar around her.

She pushed forward. "Ani's not a thief," she shouted. "He can't tell you where the mirror is because he doesn't know. You must find the real thief."

"Keep quiet," Opet warned her and gripped her arm. She shrugged her off and ran forward again.

"The sentence is death," Nakhte read from his papyrus. "When the moon is full, in accordance with the laws of the Pharaohs, you will be killed, and your body will be put in a sack and thrown into the river."

The river where she'd sailed with Ani on feast days, and where crocodiles lurked below the surface. Ani all alone in the dark depths of the water, lost forever to the Underworld.

"No," she screamed again. "No, no, no." She shoved forward, beating her fists against the medjay who blocked her way.

"Stand back," the guard said, as she squirmed in his grasp. Then she felt the slap of a hand sting her face, slamming her down, as she heard her father shout her name.

"Teti."

The moon swung back into the middle of the sky, and the stars came into focus. Gradually Rashida became aware of the sounds of the night, the dogs in the distance and a mosquito whining. And nearby, Mum's even breathing.

She lay rigid for several minutes, the voice of the scribe echoing in her ears and, over and over, the screams of the girl. She tried to blank the cries out, but they wouldn't go away. She bit her lip, blinking back the tears which suddenly filled her eyes. She knew how the girl was feeling. Afraid and lonely.

She swallowed the lump in her throat, and thought back to the scene in the courtroom. What was it the girl had cried?

"He can't tell you where the mirror is, because he doesn't know."

The words came back in a rush. A shiver ran down her spine, and her hands went cold, as she realised what they meant.

"I've got it," she wanted to scream, so loudly that her voice would break through the barrier of the centuries. "I've got the mirror. It's here."

But the mirror in her hand stayed blank. The girl, Teti, had gone, and around Rashida the shadows turned into crocodile jaws and the moon was almost full.

CHAPTER NINE

"What's that on your face?" Mum asked the next morning, as they sat drinking sweet, milky tea together. The sun was already hot, and it was going to be another burning day.

"It looks like a bruise," she added, turning Rashida's head towards the light to get a better view. "Have you been fighting?"

Rashida's mouth dropped open. For a second, she stared at Mum unable to move. Fear washed over her in long, cold waves.

The dream was coming true.

"What is it?" asked Mum. "What's the matter?" She reached over and pulled Rashida towards her and stroked her curls. Rashida closed her eyes for a moment and leant back against Mum's shoulder.

She almost told her everything then. All about the mirror, and Teti and Ani, and the trial and the crocodiles waiting in the river. "It's . . ." she started to say, then remembered Sami, and the lies she had told. Her voice wavered and fell silent. She couldn't tell Mum. It would be like telling Sami too. They'd take the mirror away and she wouldn't see it again.

She shook her head slightly. "I'm fine," she said, pulling away. She grabbed her school uniform and marched into the bathroom. She could sense Mum's eyes following her as she banged the door behind her, but she didn't look back.

Rashida hunched over the basin and tried to stop shivering. Things like this just didn't happen. Not in real life. She almost laughed out loud. Real?

She pinched herself, to make sure she was still there, and not some spirit from the past, then put her face close up to the bathroom cabinet on the wall. She looked at the purple stain that spread down the side of her face. Mum was right. It was a bruise.

She traced its outline with her finger, her mind going back to the trial. She heard the girl's cries again, then the slap as the guard's hand whipped against her cheek. Rashida cringed at the memory, then, as her eyes focused on the bruise again, she almost shouted out loud.

No wonder she had a mark on the side of her face. She'd fallen asleep with her cheek on the mirror.

Relief flooded through her and she propped herself against the wall to stop herself collapsing.

That was the last time she was going to look in the mirror and let herself be frightened out of her wits. She'd put it back where she'd found it.

She'd . . . she'd give it to Sami and forget all about it.

She splashed water on her face a couple of times, feeling as if a load had slipped off her shoulders and she was free again. "How could I be so silly?" she muttered angrily to herself as she squeezed the toothpaste out and began to brush her teeth.

"Are you going to be in there all day long?" Grandma rattled the door handle, making her jump.

"Coming," Rashida said. She rinsed her mouth, and wiped her face, then started getting dressed.

She was almost ready when her eye caught the toothbrush again, and she paused. Sea green. Sea green like the girl's eyes, the first time she had seen them, brimful of tears. As if asking for help.

Rashida frowned, angrily dragging a comb through her curls, wincing as it snagged on a knot. She shut her eyes to get rid of the image of Teti, but it wouldn't go away. She could almost hear her now, calling: "Help, please help."

Rashida shook away the thought. Teti couldn't be calling, she reminded herself, because she wasn't even real. She had died, if she ever existed, three thousand years ago, hadn't she? Except . . .

Rashida shoved her comb back into the cabinet, and leant wearily against the wall. Her head began to ache, and she wanted to crawl back to bed and forget the questions that whirled around inside her.

It was all so mixed up, as if time itself was in a muddle. If Teti was alive, then her father really was going to die unless they found the mirror. But the mirror was lying upstairs on the roof, and there was no way she could get it back to them.

Rashida frowned at the idea that crossed her mind. It was crazy. But the more she thought about it, the clearer it became. Perhaps she was meant to find the mirror. She was supposed to help. The only problem was working out how.

"Rashida," Grandma banged on the door again. "I want to use the bathroom now."

"Almost finished," Rashida answered hastily, pulling

her school tunic over her head.

Mum was preparing beans when Rashida emerged.

"It sounds like Grandma got out of bed on the wrong side this morning," she smiled. She handed Rashida a plate and a piece of bread.

Rashida said nothing. She'd managed to avoid Grandma last night, but she would have to talk to her soon, before she said anything to Mum.

"Don't forget we've been invited to Abla Fawzia's for lunch," said Mum, sitting down opposite her.

"I haven't," said Rashida. Mum was going to walk to school with her, and meet up with Sami and show him Abu Nuwaif.

Silence settled between them, but it was a comfortable morning silence.

"Do you believe in people coming back from the past?" Rashida asked after a bit.

"You mean ghosts?" said Mum, looking surprised. "Why?"

"Just wondering," murmured Rashida, scooping up some beans with a piece of flat bread. "Why do . . . ghosts appear?"

"They're supposed to be people who died unhappy," said Mum. "I think they're the result of people having over-active imaginations."

Rashida chewed steadily, silently phrasing her next question.

"Supposing something bad happened in the past," she began slowly. "Could we help change it?"

"Of course not," said Mum. "What's past is past." She

looked closely at Rashida. "Is this about Dad?" she asked.

"No," Rashida said quickly. "Someone was just talking at school. That's all."

Mum looked as if she didn't believe her.

"Honestly," said Rashida.

"Come on," said Mum, after a short silence. She looked at her watch. "We can't change the past, but we can stop the bad in the future. If we hurry, you won't get a detention for being late."

Rashida forced herself to smile but her mind was on the other girl, and it seemed to her as they walked along the road that, somewhere nearby, she was watching and waiting.

CHAPTER TEN

"What's the matter, Sami?" asked Abla Fawzia, leaning across the low, round table. It was later that afternoon and they were having lunch at her house. The table was crowded with dishes of food – lamb and green beans, grilled chicken, roast pigeon, rice, salad and bread. "Don't you like my cooking?" she went on. "You've hardly touched a thing."

Rashida watched Sami through half-closed eyes, enjoying his discomfiture. If she hadn't hated him so much, she might have felt sorry for him. He'd been eating for the last half hour and had been forced to loosen his trouser belt.

"It's delicious," he mumbled. "But I'm full, honestly."

Mum should have warned him, thought Rashida. Abla Fawzia never took 'no' for an answer, especially when it came to food.

She and Mum had been at school together and, at that

time, so Mum said, they'd been the same size. Rashida could never quite believe it when she looked at them now. Mum was as thin as a corn stalk, and Abla Fawzia as round as a football.

"Have a bit more then," Abla Fawzia said again, cutting off a leg of chicken and passing it over to Sami. "Don't be shy with me. You're marrying my best friend."

Sami smiled weakly, and toyed with the chicken. Rashida knew just how he felt. She was stuffed to bursting herself, and could barely move.

"And what about you, Rashida?" Abla Fawzia suddenly turned on her and, before she could refuse, had heaped more rice on her plate.

"You won't grow properly if you eat like that," she clucked in disapproval. "Now get that down you."

Rashida glanced up in horror, and caught Sami smiling at her. He winked and she found herself grinning in return. Until she realised what she was doing and looked quickly away.

For the rest of the afternoon, she avoided him, and was glad when they got up to go.

Abla Fawzia lived near the mosque, where men were already gathering for evening prayers, washing their hands and feet at the taps outside. The square was full. The café was crowded. A row of men sat outside puffing on nargileh pipes, and from inside came the noise of people playing cards.

They turned down the main street, past the school. Friends of Mum stopped them constantly, eyeing Sami covertly as they shook hands and said hello.

Rashida had to admit that Iman was right. As far as looks went, Sami wasn't that bad. He didn't smell or spit. He was also taller than Mum and, except for the moustache, almost handsome.

The sun was setting as they left the village. The first stars were pinpricks of light in the sky.

"Just think," said Sami. "In Cairo right now, the roads are blocked with traffic jams and you can't hear yourself speak for the noise." They crossed a small bridge over a ditch. "Why don't we build a house here?"

Rashida shot him a quick look. How dare he joke about things like that, she thought angrily. But he looked quite serious.

And suddenly Rashida had an image of them living in a new house near Grandma's. She shook her head quickly to get rid of the thought. If she wasn't careful, she'd be calling Sami 'Dad' before tomorrow.

They were nearly home. The moon was rising, almost fully round like a silver coin. Everything was very still.

"The Ancient Egyptians believed the moon was one of the eyes of the God Horus," said Sami. "They believed he'd been in a fight and his eye was ripped out. As the moon gets bigger like now, it's his eye getting better."

Mum laughed. "Two more days to go and he'll be fine again," she said.

Rashida stopped dead in her tracks, the words resounding in her brain. Mum's and Sami's voices faded away and instead she heard the scribe, addressing Ani, as clearly as if he was standing beside her.

"In two days' time when the moon is full, you will be killed, and your body will be put in a sack and thrown into the river."

Rashida drew in her breath sharply and looked at the almost round moon. She shivered, as the meaning sank in. Time marching in parallel. Two days until a full moon in Teti's time. Two days in her own.

Just forty-eight hours. If she was going to help, she would have to do something fast. She looked up at the moon again, but there were no answers in the evening sky, no way of telling her how to solve a three thousand-year-old problem with all the laws of science stacked against her.

"Car coming," Mum called. Rashida moved to the side of the road. A truck jolted past, raising a cloud of dust. Rashida started walking again, her mind made up now. She'd find an answer somehow. She had to.

CHAPTER ELEVEN

Rashida turned her back on Iman's house with a sigh of relief. She'd left Mum and Grandma behind, gossiping under the mango tree. It was already the next evening. It had been impossible to get a minute to herself all day. The mirror had hung heavy in her bag at her side. She'd been unable to escape with it even for a second.

Mum and Grandma had looked at her curiously when she said she was leaving, but had accepted the excuse of homework. Iman hadn't been so easily satisfied. "What's the matter with you these days?" she'd complained. "You're acting really strangely, and Sami's not even here." Sami had gone to the café in the village with Iman's father and Uncle Muhammed.

Rashida had just shrugged. "Do what you want then," Iman had said as she picked up her baby brother and turned away. "I don't care."

But Rashida felt Iman's eyes following her as she walked away from the house and along the path that led the short distance home. She wanted to turn back and explain. To tell Iman about the mirror and Teti and the questions that were going round and round in her head in a ceaseless muddle. But it would be no good. Iman wouldn't understand. She had to do this on her own.

It was getting dark when she arrived home. She flicked on the light in the bedroom and fell on to the nearest bed. Then she pulled her bag towards her and took out the mirror.

After a couple of minutes, her attention wandered. Something was wrong. She couldn't work it out at first. Her eyes moved round the room, taking in the half-open shutters and the pile of books which lay higgledy-piggledy on the windowsill.

Mum's green dress lay screwed up on the floor. One of the drawers was half open, scarves draped over the edge.

Rashida felt slightly uneasy. Mum was the tidiest person she knew. It wasn't like her to leave things in a jumble.

Rashida sat up and looked around again, slowly. The two beds looked normal at first glance, but then she noticed how the blue sheets were ruffled and untucked, and one of the pillows was askew. When she moved across to inspect the clothes hanging on the wall pegs, she jabbed her leg against a suitcase. It had been pulled out from under the bed and not pushed back again.

Rashida sat down slowly on the bed.

"I'm imagining things," she said out loud. It made her feel better to hear her voice. "No-one's going to break into Grandma's. There's nothing to steal. Mum was in a hurry. That's all."

She lay back on the bed and tried to concentrate on Teti again, but her unease wouldn't go away. There was one place, she thought, that Mum and Grandma would never touch without her special permission. She leant forward and pulled open the little drawer in the bedside table. This was where she kept her special things: a picture of Dad on a felucca boat, the necklace Mum had given her last Eid, and what she grandly called her diary but which was in fact an old exercise book.

The drawer was in a mess. Rashida stared down at the jumble, her hands cold. She wasn't imagining this. Someone had been there. And it wasn't Mum.

Her eyes fell on the mirror and her stomach gave a sudden lurch. For an awful moment, she thought she was going to be sick.

Someone had been searching for the mirror. For a second, she thought it might be Grandma who'd grown fed up of waiting for her to tell the truth. But Grandma would never do something like this. Never sneak in here behind her back.

There was only one other person. Someone who wanted the mirror, who had been interested in it, from the very beginning. Sami.

Rashida swallowed hard. She'd never liked him, but she had never thought he was a thief. He must have slipped back here from the café, thinking he would have the place to himself. She could imagine him creeping up to the house, glancing over his shoulder to check there was no-one about, turning the handle of the door and pushing it open.

A sound from outside interrupted her train of thought. She froze. Someone was walking across the courtyard. She could hear the 'tap tap' of footsteps crossing the tiles.

Sami was still in the house. Of course, she must have disturbed him. And now he'd seen the light on and was coming to get her.

She stared at the light bulb, transfixed. Her heart

roared in her ears as loud as a zar drum. She should be running to safety, out across the fields where she could bury herself among the maize, but she couldn't move.

The footsteps stopped. She held her breath, clutching the mirror tightly against her chest.

"Hello? Is anyone at home?"

Rashida let the mirror fall, relief flooding over her. It was Abla Selma, of all people. Rashida jumped up and ran outside, for once pleased to see her.

Abla Selma was standing by the door to the salon. She turned in surprise. "I'm sorry," she said. "I thought the house was empty. I . . . ." She hesitated. "I was looking for your mother."

"She's still over at Iman's," Rashida said.

"Can you tell her I called?" said Abla Selma, moving towards the front door. She paused, taking in Rashida's appearance. "Are you all right?"

"Have you seen Sami?" Rashida blurted out.

"Where? Here?" Abla Selma sounded surprised. "No, I don't think so. Why? Is something wrong?"

"He's been snooping round my room." The words were out before Rashida could stop them.

Abla Selma looked startled.

"You must be imagining things," she said. "Why would he do that?"

Rashida shook her head. She didn't want to talk about the mirror.

"It can't be easy for you at the moment," Abla Selma said slowly, "but you mustn't go round saying things like that."

She reached the front door, then stopped and looked back.

"Rashida," she said, then paused as if she didn't know how to go on. "Listen, if you have any problems, remember you can always come and talk to me."

Rashida watched her as she walked away, and wondered what she'd really meant to say. It was only a feeling, but she had the impression that Abla Selma didn't like Sami either. It was some comfort.

CHAPTER TWELVE

The next day dawned. Rashida lay on her side, watching the red circle of the sun as it inched its way over the low wall that surrounded the roof. Mum lay fast asleep beside her, and from downstairs came the steady roar of Grandma's snores.

It hurt Rashida to look at Mum. For some reason she couldn't understand, she'd said nothing to Mum the night before. She had tidied up the room and, when Sami had brought Mum home, she'd tried to pretend that everything was normal. She'd even managed to speak to Sami before he left for the hotel. And if Mum had noticed that she was extra quiet, she hadn't said anything.

It should be a moment of victory, Rashida thought. There was no way Mum would marry Sami, not when Rashida told her what he had done. But it didn't make her feel good. Instead, she felt like crying.

She sighed and felt under her pillow for the mirror. She pulled it out, then got quietly to her feet and, picking up her sandals, tiptoed down the stone steps and across the courtyard. The front door squeaked as she opened it. She paused for a second, then slipped outside. She didn't have long. Grandma would be up soon.

Rashida dragged an old wooden box under the lemon tree and sat down on it. Then she balanced the mirror between her hands. She had tried to look for Teti the night before, but her heart hadn't been in it. She hadn't been able to get Sami's face out of her mind, and the mirror had stayed as smooth and as blank as Grandma's washing up bowl.

"Teti," she whispered urgently now. "Teti."

She waited, frowning fiercely down at her own reflection.

"Teti," she whispered again. "Tell me what you want me to do."

The cock put its head back and started crowing. Rashida waved her hand at it impatiently.

She turned back to the mirror, and held her breath as her reflection gradually dissolved. Grew black as night. She was engulfed in thick, foul-smelling air, and felt as though she was drowning.

The girl stood trembling in the hot, stinking darkness, clutching the blue bead she wore round her neck.

Her skin crawled. She wanted to turn away and ask the guard to let her out into the daylight. Something brushed against her leg, and she stuffed her hand into her mouth to stop herself screaming.

Her father stirred and touched her arm.

Her lip trembled, but she swallowed the lump in her throat, and forced herself to speak. "Here's some water," she whispered, pushing the clay pitcher into his hand.

She felt him take it, but he didn't drink. Instead he pulled her down beside him on the floor.

"Teti," he croaked. "I want you to listen. You must be good. Be obedient and work hard, when I am gone. Opet will look after you. You will live with her and do

*what she tells you. At heart, she is a good woman,
despite her tongue."*

*"You won't die," the girl burst out. "I won't let you.
I'll find the real thief."*

*"It's too late," her father said. "The moon is
growing large."*

*"I've made offerings at the temple to the god of
justice. I'll speak to Nakhte. I'll beg him to help us.
They will listen to him."*

*"He can do nothing. There is the proof of the
amulet."*

*The man was silent again. Teti reached out and
held his hand.*

*"Is there nothing you can tell me?" she asked. "Did
you see anything that night when you were walking?"*

Ani was silent for a long time.

*"There was a figure on the path near the temple,"
Ani said finally. "At first, I thought it was the temple
guard, but it moved like someone who did not want to
be seen."*

"Where did it go?" asked Teti.

*"It disappeared," her father said, "in the direction
of the tombs."*

*"I'll watch," Teti promised. "I'll go to the temple
and watch tonight. Perhaps it'll come back."*

The darkness turned grey, turned pink. Rashida blinked
in the morning light, gulping in lungfuls of clean, fresh
air. She felt grimy all over and wanted to rush indoors
and turn on the shower as far as it would go, and wash

herself from head to toe. But not yet. She wasn't ready. She turned back to the mirror.

"Teti," she begged out loud. "What can I do?"

The mirror stayed blank. "Answer me. Tell me what to do." Rashida said desperately.

"Find the real thief." Teti's words seemed to echo through the morning air. Rashida sat bolt upright, her mind working fast. She went back over the scene again, then suddenly sucked in her breath with excitement.

"The path near the temple." There was a temple in Abu Nuwaif, or the ruins of one, near the museum. That must be what the mirror was telling her. Perhaps if she went there, she'd find out something.

Her mind raced. She would have to sneak off after school. She'd never been there on her own before. Grandma didn't like her wandering outside the village on her own. She said it would bring dishonour on the family.

Rashida hesitated, then looked up at the sun, which had climbed higher into the sky. One more day to go, she thought, and the moon would be full. She had no option.

The ruins of the temple lay at the top of the dusty brown hill behind Abu Nuwaif. The hill marked the boundary between the green of the valley and the desert, which stretched away into the distance. Rashida paused at the entrance to the temple site and looked back the way she had come. From where she stood, she could see the houses of Abu Nuwaif huddled round the mosque and the strip of green fields leading down to the river. If she screwed up her eyes, she could just make out Grandma's house, away to the right, standing on its own, and Iman's a bit further on, two specks of white in the green.

The road was empty, except for a herd of goats chewing at the thorn bushes and an old man on his donkey. He looked at her curiously and she drew back inside the gate.

She moved slowly towards the ruins. They were at the far end of the car park: a couple of bashed-about columns and bits of wall, slabs of paving stones and a rounded archway.

There was no-one else around.

Rashida stretched out her hand and cautiously traced the carving on one of the pillars. It was rough and warm from the sun. A brown lizard gulped at her, then darted away and disappeared.

She shivered in spite of the heat.

The old people in the village told stories about the spirits that lived in the temple. If you listened hard at night, they said, you could hear them shrieking. Grandma said it was the wind howling and not to be stupid. But Rashida wasn't so sure.

She closed her eyes and tried to imagine the temple busy with priests and singing and noise. And, in the middle, Teti, clinging to Ani's hand, so as not to get lost among the worshippers.

But other pictures crowded in. Silent mummies rising from their tombs, and bony hands reaching out towards her.

"Stop being so silly," Rashida said out loud, then

gasped as jabbering voices and screeching laughter shattered the silence.

She spun round, her heart pounding somewhere up in her throat, and saw a group of tourists coming out from the museum, laughing and chattering among themselves.

She drew back behind a pillar and watched as they moved towards their bus, and climbed inside. Her attention was drawn to two men who stood slightly apart talking. The one in the blue shirt was waving his arms in the air and shouting, the other, obviously a tourist, was repeatedly shaking his head. Suddenly, they both laughed and shook hands, as if they'd come to an agreement. The tourist climbed into the bus and after a moment it drove off, towards Saida. The man in the blue shirt went back into the museum.

Silence fell again.

Rashida looked closely at the ruins, searching for a clue.

There was nothing. No blazing sign. No slippery figure emerging from behind a pillar, whispering, "I did it. I stole the mirror."

Her head was starting to ache, and she was beginning to wish she had never come.

A shadow passed over her. She looked up and saw a huge vulture circling overhead, so close to her that she could, see its cruel yellow eyes. In a sudden panic, she scrambled to her feet and, grabbing her bag, raced towards the shelter of the museum.

It was dark inside after the dazzle of the sun and, for a moment, Rashida leant against the wall, enjoying the cold, air-conditioned room. The museum was empty. There was no sign of the man in the blue shirt. Rashida was glad. She didn't want to be seen.

She looked about her, at the dusty, glass-fronted cabinets and the statues and urns along the wall. Perhaps the clue was here, dug up by some archaeologist from the temple site. Perhaps one of the bits of broken pottery, or the odd bits of metal, the papyri perhaps, or that old wooden stool. She tiptoed among the display cabinets, examining the neatly typed cards.

No, there was nothing here. Nothing except a load of old junk.

A wave of depression swept over her. She was no nearer the answer. The sun would go down in a few hours, and the moon would rise and Ani would be killed. There was nothing she could do about it.

She emerged blinking into the bright sunlight and started walking towards the exit, casting a final look at the temple ruins.

Then she saw Sami.

He was standing framed in the temple arch, deep in conversation with the man from the museum. She drew back behind a wall, not wanting to be seen, and peered out at him.

The sun caught his face sideways on, and bronzed and sharpened it. He was smiling as he scribbled something on the rolled-up newspaper he held in his hand. It looked like the papyri she had seen in the museum. Her hand gripped the wall in front of her and her mind did somersaults.

It wasn't Sami's face she could see now, but Nakhte's. Nakhte, the scribe, smiling as he scratched on the papyrus, his face caught in a shaft of sunlight. Just like Sami's smile the first time she had met him. Their faces fitted one on top of the other. So like each other that Rashida caught her breath in surprise.

She forced herself to move. She had to get away before she was seen. She dashed across to the gate, then peered back to take another look at Sami.

She shivered. It was as if Nakhte had come chasing across the centuries to get the mirror back again.

Her eyes widened as she realised what it meant. It was the sign she'd been looking for.

Nakhte was the thief.

CHAPTER THIRTEEN

Rashida awoke to her darkened room, her head still thumping painfully. It was hot and the sweat had trickled down, making the sheet damp. The afternoon light seeped in through the shutters, creating patterns on the wall. From outside she could hear the murmur of voices.

She had fallen asleep almost as soon as she got home. Grandma had taken one look at her pale face and sent her off to bed with a glass of helba, instead of a lecture for being late. There had been no sign of Sami, and he hadn't passed her as she ran home.

Rashida turned and looked at the clock. Four o'clock. The moon would be rising in a couple of hours.

Panic spurted inside her again. She pulled the mirror out from under her pillow and tried to concentrate, tried to will Teti out of the past, as she'd done before.

She had to tell Teti about Nakhte. She had to warn her. Her head throbbed. Nakhte. Sami. The pain thumped and banged behind her eyes, so she could hardly see.

She screwed up her eyes, but images took over her mind. Nakhte, Sami. Sami, Nakhte. Their faces revolved in her brain, spinning faster and faster, until they fused into one horrid, leering grimace and she couldn't tell one from the other.

She let the mirror drop.

It was after seven when she opened her eyes again. Mum was standing at the door with a glass in her hand, and it was dark outside.

"Come on, sleepy-head," she said. "I've made you some mint tea."

She put the glass down and came and sat on the bed. "Feeling better?" she asked, as she stroked Rashida's forehead. Rashida nodded.

"Go and have a shower," said Mum, "then come and join us. There's something we've got to talk about."

"What is it?" Rashida asked, aware for the first time how serious Mum looked.

"Get up and you'll see," was all she said, pulling her upright.

Rashida tottered off into the bathroom, wondering what the matter was. She shut the door behind her, then turned on the water, and let it splash all over her. She could hear the rumble of voices, coming from the sitting room. Men's voices. She clenched her fists.

Sami was back. And that meant only one thing.

He must have seen her at the museum and told Grandma and Mum. She was in for the biggest telling off of her life. Another thought flashed into her mind. She'd be kept in all evening. She'd have no chance of contacting Teti. She had to think of some excuse. Her mind raced over possibilities – a school project, a look-alike, an errand for Abla Selma.

She rubbed herself dry and put on a clean gallabia, which smelt of Sunlight soap. There was a sinking feeling in her stomach as she walked across the brown and white tiles of the courtyard and into the sitting room.

The first person she saw was the man from the museum. He was still wearing the blue shirt he'd had on earlier that day, and, when he rose to his feet, she smelt the faint whiff of perfume.

"Salam alaikum," Rashida murmured automatically, as she shook his hand.

She slid a glance at Mum, then over at Grandma, who was sitting, slightly bent, contemplating the floor. Finally, she looked at Sami.

He was sitting beside Mum, smiling to himself as he turned and twisted something in his big, powerful hands.

For a second, Rashida's head whirled. Black spots danced in front of her eyes and she had to put her hand against the wall to steady herself.

Then her mind cleared.

"What are you doing with my mirror?" she demanded.

Mum broke the silence. "I took it while you were asleep," she explained. "I should have asked, I know, but we had to show it to Ustaz Nuri." She gestured towards the man in the blue shirt. "He's the Antiquities Inspector."

Rashida could feel the tension in the air, and her head started thumping again.

"Where exactly did you find it?" Ustaz Nuri asked.

"I bought it," Rashida answered defiantly. "From the market. I've already told them." She jerked her head at Mum and Sami.

"We know that's not true," Mum said. "Grandma's told us how you found it."

Rashida swivelled round. Grandma was sitting upright, against the wall, in her old black gallabia with the faded pink scarf knotted around her head. She had her eyes closed and was fingering her beads.

Rashida could feel the tears welling up from deep down inside her. She bit her lip to stop it trembling. Mum had betrayed her.

And now Grandma.

After a couple of moments she realised Mum was still talking. "Luckily for you, Sami recognised it straight away for what it was," she said. "If the antiquities people had found out that you'd discovered something and kept it, you would have been in serious trouble. We all would have been." She turned to the inspector. "She's just a school girl," she apologised. "She didn't realise."

Rashida gasped. They were going to take the mirror away from her and she'd never see it again.

She flashed a look at Ustaz Nuri, remembering how she'd last seen him, shaking hands with that tourist. Now she came to think about it, how did they know he was really an antiquities inspector? It was suddenly all quite clear. He was in it with Sami. They were going to take the mirror away from her and sell it on the black market.

"You c-can't let him have it," she stammered.

"They'll be very careful with it," said Sami.

Rashida ignored him. She could feel her legs shaking and a thick mass forming in the pit of her stomach, in which all the anger and fear and pain of the last few days were jumbled up together.

The words streamed out. "Sami's lying," she said. "He and this man are in it together. I saw them up at the museum, doing a deal with the tourists. They're going to

76

sell the mirror on the black market."

She was aware of Mum staring at her tight-lipped and pale-faced, but she couldn't stop.

"Sami . . ." she struggled to find the right word. "Sami burgled my room the other day. He's just a thief." She finished.

There was a deadly silence. Grandma was looking angrier than Rashida had ever seen her before. Sami started to speak, telling them not to worry, that he was sure Ustaz Nuri would understand.

But Grandma interrupted him. "Rashida will apologise right this minute," she said in a cold voice Rashida had never heard before.

"No," Rashida said. "No, I won't. I'm telling the truth. You'll see." Then she grabbed the mirror from Sami and tore out of the room, before anyone could stop her.

The full moon was rising when she got outside, a perfect silver circle in the sky.

She glanced up at it in desperation. She still had the mirror, but time was running out. She headed for the field of maize, her thoughts racing. She had to get away, and fast. Somewhere where she could think and work out what to do, and where no-one could find her. She'd go to Iman's. No, that would be the first place they would think of looking.

She dived in amongst the corn stalks, and crouched there, trembling. Something rustled nearby, and she froze, thinking of the snake that had been killed there last month. She couldn't stay here all night.

From behind her, she could hear Sami shouting. His words were carried away in the cool evening breeze, but they sounded like a curse.

Rashida crept deeper into the corn.

Then she remembered Abla Selma. "If you ever need anyone to talk to," she'd said, "you can always come to me."

She'd go to Abla Selma's. At least she'd be safe there.

CHAPTER FOURTEEN

Rashida collapsed against Abla Selma's front door, and knocked as loud as she dared. She was out of breath, and her knee hurt where she had fallen and grazed it.

She knocked again, and heard the sound of footsteps and a key being turned in the lock.

"Rashida?" Abla Selma said in surprise. "What on earth are you doing out at this time of night, and on your own?"

"You've got to help me," Rashida gasped. "It's Sami. He's trying to steal my mirror. He's going to sell it to some tourists."

She gulped then went on. "He's a thief. Mum's going to marry a thief." Then she burst into tears.

Abla Selma opened the door wide. "You'd better come in," she said, and ushered Rashida into the tidy sitting room.

Rashida sat down on a chair, feeling awkward and dirty. Her feet were covered in dust and her hands were grimy.

"Why don't I make us a drink, while you get your breath back," Abla Selma said, "and then we'll see what we can do."

"You won't let Sami in, will you?" Rashida asked. "He's evil."

Abla Selma shook her head. "Don't worry," she said, before leaving the room. "No-one's going to hurt you."

Rashida tried to stop shaking. She could see the

moon through the window, rising higher in the sky. Teti. She must try again, she must warn her.

She held the mirror up to her face. "Teti," she whispered. "Please come. Please, please."

From the kitchen came the sound of Abla Selma running water into a kettle. Rashida relaxed. She still had a couple of minutes. She glanced round the room at the artefacts Abla Selma had on display and her books on Ancient Egypt.

Then she looked down at the mirror, and felt her heart starting to thump as the picture emerged, dark and indistinct. She peered closer and saw it was night with the pinpricks of starlight and the silver glow of the moon.

Teti crouched down on the ground near the temple, keeping watch.

It was her last chance. At dawn they would kill Ani and dump his body in the river. She closed her eyes to shut away the thought. A rat scuttled nearby and a dog howled somewhere in the darkness. She shivered and huddled closer to the ground.

Then she saw the movement.

It was so slight at first that she thought she had imagined it, a breeze rustling a tree, a bat winging its way home.

Then she saw it again, a shadow slipping down the path that went past the tombs and on down to where the river gleamed silver in the moonlight.

She strained her eyes in the darkness, holding her breath, searching for the movement. For a while there was nothing, then she caught it again: a figure gliding from one pool of darkness to another, too far away to see properly.

The girl set off in pursuit. The path was rocky and uneven. She dislodged a pebble. The rattle of the stone sounded like thunder in the still night air. She froze against the side of the hill, and waited, then moved on again. Down, down until the path had left the barren hill and was weaving among the wheat fields.

Ahead, the figure glided forward, no longer stopping and starting, no longer checking behind.

Teti crept forward, nearer and nearer. Until she reached the trees that grew right by the riverside. Then she halted.

It was easy to see the figure now, bright white in the moonlight. Down by the date palm, scrabbling in the dirt. It was easy to recognise her.

Teti shivered.

She'd seen her so many times before, bending over the trays of loaves in the bakery, standing behind her in the courtroom.

Opet, her father's cousin, was squatting at the base of the tree, wiping the earth away from something that gleamed in the moonlight.

The mirror darkened and the figures disappeared. For a brief moment, the image of the palm tree lingered on, then it too faded into nothingness, and Rashida was left with the sound of her own rapid breathing.

She leant back in the wooden chair and stared down at the mirror, her mind a muddle of 'don't understand's and 'why's and 'what's.

Nakhte hadn't stolen the mirror. It had been Opet all along. Rashida twisted the mirror in her hands. She'd been wrong about everything – about the thief, and helping Teti, and there being a reason for it all. She put the mirror down on a nearby table. She should be happy now.

Everything would be all right. Teti had found the thief, and Ani would be safe. She'd hand the mirror over to the proper authorities and Grandma would be satisfied.

Except . . . she glanced down at the mirror again.

For a second, Teti's eyes seemed to gaze back at her. "Don't leave me," she seemed to be saying. "Wait."

Rashida started as Abla Selma came back into the room carrying a tray, which she placed on the table in the middle.

"I've made us some tea," she said. "Now sit down and tell me what this is all about."

Rashida took the cup numbly, and sipped the strong black tea, forcing her mind back to the present.

"Sami says the mirror's from Ancient Egypt," she began. She squinted over at Abla Selma, wondering how to go on. "He tried to steal it, and now he's brought along a man whom he claims is an Antiquities Inspector, and who says I've got to give it up. But I know they're really planning to sell it to some tourists."

Rashida knew she wasn't making much sense, and half expected Abla Selma to rap on the table with a ruler

82

and tell her to take a detention. Perhaps it had been a mistake coming here after all.

She picked up the mirror and got up to go. "I . . . I'm sorry," she mumbled. "I shouldn't have disturbed you."

"Don't be silly," said Abla Selma. "I'm glad you've come. Now let me see this famous mirror."

Rashida didn't give it to her immediately.

"I see pictures in it," she blurted out suddenly. "From the past. There's a girl called Teti whose father's going to be killed because they think he stole the mirror from the tomb. But it wasn't him. It was Opet, his cousin. They trusted her."

The words streamed out. Rashida was vaguely aware of Abla Selma perched on the edge of her chair listening, not laughing.

"I thought it was Nakhte," Rashida rushed on. "But I should have known. I saw the figure, near the palm tree. I saw Opet."

She stopped as the words sank in. Her mind shifted back to the moments after the sandstorm, seeing again the figure bent double beside the tree. She frowned in concentration.

"What's the matter?" Abla Selma prompted.

Rashida shook her head. She was still trying to make sense of it. It was as if everything was turning full circle and she was back at the beginning again.

"I'm not sure," she said. "I think I've got to go to the palm tree." She rose slowly to her feet.

"What do you mean?" asked Abla Selma. "What palm tree?"

"I have to be there," Rashida struggled to explain. "Teti's waiting for me," she said.

"You're not going anywhere at this time of the night," said Abla Selma, sharply. "Not with that mirror. Now, let me see it." She held out her hand.

It was thin and scrawny like a bird's claw. Rashida's eyes focused on it, as if she were seeing it for the first time. She felt herself go cold.

"Let me have the mirror," said Abla Selma, again. Her voice had changed. It had lost its patience, and was high with excitement, an excitement that made Rashida nervous. She looked around the room, and took in again the artefacts and books on Ancient Egypt.

She backed away, horror dawning in her eyes as the pieces suddenly fell into place in her mind. She remembered the greedy way Abla Selma had held on to the mirror, the night of the party; and the way she'd stood fumbling for words that other night, pretending she'd come to see Mum, when all the time it was *she* who'd been rifling through Rashida's room.

Not Sami, but Abla Selma. "If you ever want to talk," she'd said then, "come and see me." And Rashida had walked right into her trap.

Rashida took a step backwards, her eyes fixed on the teacher, suddenly afraid. Her mouth had gone dry, and she could feel her heart starting to pound.

"You," she whispered. "It was you in my room."

Then she turned and ran, knocking over a table in her haste to get out of the room.

84

"Wait!" shouted Abla Selma, behind her. "You mustn't leave. Not now."

But Rashida didn't listen.

She slammed the front door behind her and raced out into the cool night air.

CHAPTER FIFTEEN

Rashida clutched the mirror close to her chest as she ran. Her mind was as cool and as clear as the rain in winter. She knew what she had to do now, where she had to go. "Don't worry, Teti," she whispered into the warm night. "I've got the mirror safe. I'm coming. Just wait for me."

She ran down the path to the gate and out past Abla Selma's old car and on to the street that ran along beside the school. She followed the school wall, round past the empty playground and the locked school gates.

Abla Selma, a thief. She could still hardly believe it. She was a teacher. She'd been invited to their house. She was even a friend of Mum's.

Rashida paused to catch her breath, as the meaning gradually sank in. If Abla Selma had searched her room, then Sami was innocent. He wasn't a thief. He hadn't been trying to trick her. He'd been telling her the truth.

Which meant, she grimaced, which meant there was nothing to stop him marrying Mum.

For a second she was furious all over again then, suddenly, she was glad. She felt as if a huge burden had dropped off her shoulders, and left her as light as air.

"Rashida. Come back!" Abla Selma's voice suddenly broke through the silence.

Rashida quickly drew back into the shadow of the wall and looked over her shoulder. Abla Selma was standing under the rickety street lamp, peering into the darkness.

"Rashida," she called again.

Rashida pressed back against the wall. The street was empty, the shops shuttered and closed and the pavements deserted. There was no-one else about.

"I'm sorry I frightened you," shouted Abla Selma. "I just want the mirror to be safe. That's all." She stood in the pool of light, looking up and down the street, and listening.

The seconds ticked slowly by. Rashida wanted to run, but her legs were paralysed. Her heart was beating so loudly she was sure that Abla Selma would hear it.

But suddenly the teacher turned away, and walked round the corner and out of sight.

Rashida waited. It was a trick, she thought, a way to force her out into the open. Minutes went by. Still nothing happened. Finally, Rashida cautiously edged out of the shadow and into the open. She hesitated a fraction longer, then raced off along the street, past the mosque and into the market square.

"Malik ya binti? What's the matter?" Sheikh Ali called out from the empty coffee shop, where he was locking up. He raised his hands and stood directly in front of her, like a traffic policeman on market day.

Rashida swerved round him. She caught a brief glimpse of his astonished face in the light that spilled out from the café, and prayed he hadn't recognised her.

"Hey," he shouted again, but she ignored him and rushed on. He was too old to run after her. He shouted something else, then his voice faded as she turned out of the square onto the road that led out of the village.

At first the houses were pressed close together. She could hear the muffled sound of voices and television, and felt reassured by the presence of these unseen people. Then the houses grew further apart, as she reached the edge of the village, and she was totally on her own.

She shivered. A stitch in her side throbbed steadily and her knee hurt where she had grazed it earlier. For a second, she considered carrying straight on, following the road round, home to Grandma and Mum.

But Teti was waiting for her and time was running out.

"Come on," she muttered out loud. "You can do it."

She could just make out the path that branched off to the left. She ran down the bank, wincing as she stubbed her toe on a stone. She was almost there. She could see the date palm, straight ahead, its ghostly outline sketched against the sky. She stopped for a second, and bent double, struggling to regain her breath.

The noise of the car took her by surprise. The roar of its engine shattered the stillness, and she looked back sharply. The car headlights sliced through the darkness. The car drew closer, and the light dazzled her. She crouched down, waiting for it to drive by.

But it didn't. It stopped, right where the path turned off to the river. There was a sudden silence, then a car door banged.

With a start of fear, Rashida recognised Abla Selma coming down the bank towards her.

For a second, Rashida stayed motionless. Then she struggled off down the path.

"Rashida, wait." Abla Selma called.

Rashida looked over her shoulder. Abla Selma was coming after her, pushing her way through the corn stalks that grew close on either side.

"You can't have it," Rashida yelled, with all the strength she could muster. "I'm going to return it, and you're not going to stop me."

Rashida staggered to the palm tree, and leant panting against it, eyes closed. I've managed it, she thought. I've got here.

She straightened up and looked about her.

She wasn't sure what she'd expected. Teti and Opet waiting for her in the flesh. A roll of thunder, or a flash of lightning. Voices, noise, movement.

The moon was so bright that she could see the tufts of grass, the round shapes of pebbles, and a dried-up palm frond.

But nothing else. She couldn't believe it.

"Teti," she whispered. "Where are you?"

There was no answer. The silence mocked her, and suddenly angry, she threw the mirror onto the ground. It clinked against a stone. Then silence fell again. A dead silence.

I'm too late, she thought miserably. I've failed. Sadness welled up inside her. She bent slowly to pick up the mirror, then spun round as someone breathed down her neck.

Abla Selma was standing right behind her. She reached out and grabbed Rashida by the arm.

"Let me go," Rashida screamed.

She tried to twist away but Abla Selma's grip was harder than she had imagined.

"Give me the mirror," she hissed.

"Leave me alone," said Rashida.

"That mirror should be mine," Abla Selma tugged at the handle. "You think it's a toy. You don't realise how precious it is. Nobody does. Nobody except me."

She was no longer the prim and proper teacher in the long, beige coat, but had a look on her face like that of a mad woman.

"I'll look after it," she crooned. "I'll care for it, like our ancestors cared for it."

She pushed Rashida back against the tree, and tightened her hold, the fingers of one hand digging deep into Rashida's arm, the other clutching at the mirror.

"Give it to me."

"I WON'T," said Rashida. She swung her right leg back, and kicked Abla Selma on the shin as hard as she was able. Abla Selma yelped in pain, and her grip slackened slightly.

Rashida wrenched herself free. Abla Selma turned on her but she was off balance, and when Rashida pushed her away with all her strength, Abla Selma fell heavily to the ground. She tried to get up, but sank back, clasping her ankle and grimacing with pain.

For the first time, Rashida was aware of other voices in the darkness, calling her name. A man's voice. Sami's. She could see the faint flicker of torchlight through the trees. He would be here any minute. She turned back to Abla Selma.

"I'm sorry," she said, as she moved away from her, to stand close to the riverbank. "You can't have the mirror, because it's not mine to give."

Then she held it up and caught her breath, as her world swung away and Teti came out of the night.

The girl grabbed Opet's arm.

"Why?" she asked. "Why are you doing this to Ani? He's done nothing wrong, and now he's going to die at sunrise because of you."

Opet's face changed. It was suddenly filled with such hatred that the girl was terrified. She's crazy, she thought.

"Good Ani," Opet sneered. "Poor Ani. I'm tired of hearing it. What about me? Who remembers me? Stupid old Opet who slaves in the bakery and cleans and cooks without a word of thanks. Well, this time, I'm the clever one. Not Ani."

"I won't tell anyone," said the girl. "I'll say I found the mirror."

Opet laughed, and twirled the mirror in her hand.

"My lovely mirror," she gloated. "I'll sell you. I'll be rich."

A sudden movement behind Opet's shoulder caught the girl's eye. A man was coming towards them quickly. It was too dark to see him clearly but she recognised his walk.

For a second she couldn't believe it, but as he drew closer, she saw it was Nakhte. The scribe must have followed her. The prison guard must have told him what Ani had said. The God of Justice had heard her prayer.

She turned in triumph to Opet.

"You can't hide," she said, pointing behind her. "Nakhte has seen you. They'll believe Ani now."

Opet's face twisted with fury.

"Not without the mirror," she said, and waved it over her head. "No," the girl cried, as she tried to snatch it. "Nakhte must have the mirror as proof."

"He's not going to believe you, now," laughed Opet, and before the girl could stop her, she threw the mirror high over her head, so high that it seemed to hang suspended in the sky.

The girl's cry reached across time. And Rashida understood.

She smoothed the surface of the mirror. For a second she didn't want to let it go. It was the most beautiful thing she had ever owned. But then she was looking at Teti, and the girl's desperate eyes stared straight into her own.

Rashida's grip on the mirror loosened. She reached out and touched the surface, and imagined the warm softness of skin. She drew her hand back, and for a brief moment smiled at Teti across the centuries. Then she tossed the mirror high into the air, watching it spin like a miniature moon.

Higher and higher it whirled, growing smaller and smaller, until it disappeared.

Rashida stared up into the darkness and saw it in her mind's eye vanishing down the long tunnel of time.

"Catch it, Teti," she whispered softly. "Catch it."

There was no reply. Just the sound of the wind sighing in the date palm and the gurgle of water as the river slipped by.

"You silly little idiot," screamed Abla Selma, crawling towards her.

Rashida said nothing.

She sank down on the ground, too tired to stand and wait for Sami and Mum to arrive and for the explanations to begin.

CHAPTER SIXTEEN

It was three days later.

Rashida and Iman sat in the shadow of the palm tree, dangling their legs over the water.

"Just think," said Iman. "No more Abla Selma."

The teacher had resigned suddenly from the school, and was gone from Abu Nuwaif, no-one quite knew where.

Rashida didn't reply.

"At least something good came out of that weird stuff," Iman said, pushing her glasses up her nose.

Rashida sighed. She had tried explaining it all, but only Grandma had really believed her.

Iman had looked at her as if she was crazy when she had talked about Teti. Mum and Sami still called it 'the accident'. They thought she had dropped the mirror by mistake when she was running from Abla Selma. Or that's what they had told the Antiquities Inspector. It had required all Sami's charm to win him round.

There had been some mention of trying to find the mirror in the river mud. But Rashida knew that would be silly. They wouldn't find anything.

It was quiet by the palm tree. The Nile flowed by on its long way to Cairo. Rashida pictured Mum and Sami, standing on a bridge, looking at the same river slipping by.

It took her a couple of seconds to realise that Iman was speaking. "What do you think of Sami now?" she asked. "If he hadn't found you, Abla Selma might have killed you."

Rashida shrugged slightly. "I don't think she would have really hurt me," she said. "She was just crazy about losing the mirror. I feel sorry for her, in a way."

Iman gaped at her, speechless.

Rashida studied her reflection in the water and considered Sami.

For a second, she felt her old jealousy sweeping over her, blotting everything else out. Then suddenly the image of Opet's face, contorted with fury, came into her mind. She shivered slightly and pushed the thought away. She didn't want to get like that.

"Sami's all right, I suppose," she said.

He had been quite understanding in the end about her suspicions of him. He'd even joked about it. Perhaps it wouldn't be too bad, him marrying Mum.

She leant back and stared up into the blue sky: so far away, there was no end to it. She thought of Teti, somewhere in another time, and wondered again.

"You'll never know," Grandma had said to her. "But you did what was right, whatever anyone else says." And she had given Rashida a quick hug.

"What's that by your hand?" Iman asked.

Rashida didn't reply at first. Iman had been making silly jokes like there'd be no tomorrow.

"I'm serious," Iman said. "There's something blue in the dust."

Rashida peered down at the ground.

She didn't know why she hadn't seen it before – a

bright blue bead in the shape of a scarab beetle. She picked it up. It felt warm, almost as if someone had been holding it for a long time before placing it there.

Her fingers closed over it and she gripped it tightly.

And somewhere in the palm trees, she thought she heard the distant laugh of a girl.

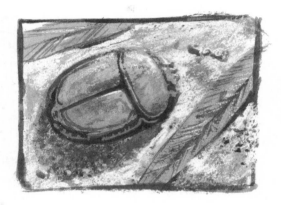